J63457

A Cake for Barney

Story by Joyce Dunbar
Pictures by Emilie Boon

ORCHARD BOOKS
New York & London
A division of Franklin Watts, Inc.

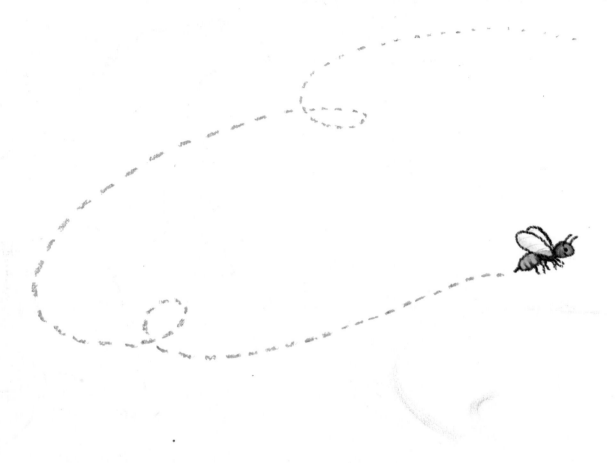

Text copyright © Joyce Dunbar 1987
Illustrations copyright © Emilie Boon 1987
First published in Great Britain in 1987 by
ORCHARD BOOKS
10 Golden Square, London W1R 3AF

Published in the United States of America in 1988 by
Orchard Books, a division of Franklin Watts, Inc.,
387 Park Avenue South, New York, NY 10016

Library of Congress Cataloging-in-Publication Data
Dunbar, Joyce.
  A cake for Barney.
  Summary: When bullies try to take his property, a young
bear learns how to stand up to them in a nonviolent way.
  [1. Bullies—Fiction.   2. Bears—Fiction.   3. Animals—Fiction]
I. Boon, Emilie, ill.   II. Title.
PZ7.D8944 Cak 1988   [E]   87-15294
ISBN 0-531-05735-6
ISBN 0-531-08335-7 (lib. bdg.)

Barney the bear had a cake.

It was a fine little cake with five
cherries on it.
Barney said to himself, "A fine little cake
with five cherries on it
will be just delicious!"
And he settled down to eat it.

But before he could take a bite,
along came a wasp. It settled right
on Barney 's nose.
"Will you please go away," said Barney,
"and let me eat my cake?"
"Yes," buzzed the wasp,
"but only if you give me a cherry."

So Barney gave the wasp a cherry.
"Oh, well," he said with a sigh,
"a fine little cake
with four cherries on it
is better than a cake with none."

He was about to take a bite
when along came a mouse in a little paper boat.
"Will you please sail away?" said Barney.
"I'm trying to eat my cake."
"Yes," squeaked the mouse, "I'll go,
but only if you give me a cherry."

So Barney gave the mouse a cherry.
"Oh, well," he said with a sigh,
"a fine little cake
  with three cherries on it
  is better than a cake with none."

He was about to take a bite
when along came a crow, croaking and cawing.
"Will you please fly away?" said Barney.
"I want to eat my cake."
"Yes," cackled the crow. "I'll go,
but only if you give me a cherry."

So Barney gave the crow a cherry.
"Oh, well," he said with a sigh,
"a fine little cake
  with two cherries on it
  is better than a cake with none."

He was about to take a bite
when along came a squirrel.
"Will you *please* go away?" said Barney.
"I'm longing to eat my cake."
"Yes," squealed the squirrel. "I'll go,
but only if you give me a cherry."

So Barney gave the squirrel a cherry.
"Oh, well," he said with a sigh,
"a fine little cake
   with one cherry on it
   is better than a cake with none."

He was about to take a bite
when along came a fox.
"Will you *please* go away?" said Barney.
"I'm *dying* to eat my cake."
"Yes," snarled the fox, "I'll go,
but only if you give me that cherry."

So Barney gave the cherry to the fox.
"Oh, well," he said with a sigh,
"a fine little cake
 with no cherries on it
 is better than no cake at all."

Then, just as he was about to take a bite,
along came a big bear named Buster.
"GO AWAY!" said Barney.
"Yes," growled Buster, "I'll go,
but only if you give me
that fine little cake."

"NO!" said Barney to Buster,
"for this fine little cake
  with no cherries on it
  is going
                going
                        going
                                going . . .

GONE!"

And it was just delicious.